Characters

SIMONE, a passionate, restless woman in her late twenties/early thirties.

TIRASOL, an anxious, determined woman in her early forties.

CAROLINE, a strong, practical, yet slightly melancholic woman in her forties.

SELAH, a woman in her fifties/early sixties. A seer.

MIRANDA, a curious and spirited woman in her late teens.

JAMIE, Simone's husband, a ghost.

Time

The present.

Setting

An open, fluid space evocative of the swamps of a burnt-out bayou.

Notes

This play should be performed without an intermission. Selected scene titles may be used for production purposes. Original songs by the author featured in the text may be performed a capella. Melodies to the songs may be obtained by contacting the author, or lyrics may be re-set by another composer.

Regarding lighting: except where indicated, there are to be no blackouts in the staging of this play. "Light change" at the end of a scene indicates a subtle but significant variance in light. "Light shift" at the end of a scene suggests a fluid shift in light, but little or no time has passed. "Lights fade" indicates a breath of rest (as in a piece of music) and denotes an elongated passage of time.

Production History

Alchemy of Desire/Dead-Man's Blues was originally developed by A.S.K. Theater

Projects, Los Angeles, and the Playwright's Center, Minneapolis. The play received its

world premiere at the Cincinnati Playhouse in the Park as winner of the Lois and

Richard Rosenthal New Play Prize (Ed Stern, Producing Artistic Director), in

Cincinnati, Ohio, on March 31, 1994. It was directed by Lisa Peterson; the set design

was by Neil Patel; the costume design was by Candice Donnelly; the lighting design

was by Mimi Jordan Sherin; the sound design was by Dan Moses Schreier and the

stage manager was Bruce E. Coyle. The play and music are also published in the

anthology *Out of the Fringe: Contemporary Latina/o Theatre and Performance* (TCG,

2000).

1.

Dark. Lights reveal Simone seated, surrounded by buckets of Kentucky Fried Chicken.

She wears a faded purple dress, and is barefoot.

SIMONE:

Chicken.

Buckets and buckets of friend chicken all over.

Twelve, sixteen, twenty-four piece…

Everybody brought one. One kind or another.

Caroline, Selah, Mrs. Hawkins…

They all came in with their chicken.

They all came in.

With their mouths open. Gristle stuck between their teeth.

Their faces smeared with grease, and perfume, and liquor.

They all came in.

Came in and flapped their arms. Calling out to God

and Jeremiah and all the powers in the universe.

They all came in with their chicken,

came in to push their thigh meat in my face.

Push it in my face to make me feel better.

I thought I'd puke.

I thought, One more bucket, I'm gonna get down on my knees

and puke right next to the coffin.

I don't like fried chicken. He sure as hell didn't.

Why'd they bring it, then? Cause that's what you do?

That what you do when somebody passes on?

Y'know, just because people been doing something a long time

don't mean you got to *keep* on doin it.

Ain't nobody said you gotta become a fool to tradition.

What didn't they bring something else?

Sweet potato pie, ice water, hard whiskey…

I wouldn't have minded some hard whiskey.

But fried chicken?

It smells up the whole house.

Smells up the house real good.

Why, you can smell the stink of the fat for miles.

… Clear up to the river, you can smell it.

Grease all over.

Goes straight through the buckets, stains the wood.

Hell to get grease out once it's stained the wood.

Fingers get oily, sticky. Hands reeking of chicken.

Grease swimming through you til *nothing*

can rid you of its reek.

Gotta get tar soap, wash it off, scrub your hands blood raw

to get rid of it.

And the thing is, who's going to eat it?

Who is going to eat the damn chicken anyway?

I can't eat it.– And he's dead.

What good's it going to do him?

Peel of the skin and fat and throw the chicken bones at him,

that's all I can do.

Bury him with the chicken bones.

Dead. He's just dead.

Some bullet ripped right through him like he was dog meat:

Eyes all busted, bones sticking out of flesh…

I didn't even recognize him.

If they didn't say it was Jamie, I wouldn't know who it was,

so little left of him that's really him.

(Sound: slightly distorted shell-fire of battle. Fade-out.)

He was my husband, Jamie was.

Damn war killed him off.

I don't even know where it was.

All I know is: one day, there was a rumor of war

and the next, he was off to some little country somewhere

I couldn't even find on a map.

And then he was dead.

We weren't even married a month.

Made love in some car, got married…

And he just *takes off.*

BASTARD.

(Sound: slightly distorted shell-fire. Fade-out.)

I can barely remember him now.

I'll see somebody, he'll look like him,

but he'll turn around and I realize he don't look like Jamie at all.

Not even married a month.

And all I got are buckets and buckets of chicken stinkin up the house.

That's all I got.

Fried chicken and a dead body.

2

Tirasol and Caroline are seated, snapping the last of a batch of beans into a large earthenware bowl. Selah and Miranda are seated to one side. Selah is fanning herself slowly. Miranda is looking out, listening. The bean snapping should serve as a kind of accompaniment to the voices—subtly, discreetly musical.

TIRASOL: You know what they say?

CAROLINE: What they say?

TIRASOL: They say she made a pile of chicken bones in her backyard.

CAROLINE: That's what they say?

TIRASOL: That's what they say.

(Beat)

Know what else they say?

CAROLINE: What they say?

TIRASOL: They say she's goin 'round without clothes on in the dead of night–

CAROLINE: No.

TIRASOL: Calling his name out like he's going to answer.

CAROLINE: They say that?

TIRASOL: I've heard it.

(Beat.)

CAROLINE: You lie.

TIRASOL: I swear on my mother's grave, may the poor woman rest in all-mighty peace.

CAROLINE: They say that?

TIRASOL: Uh-huh.

(Beat.)

CAROLINE: They sure say a lot of things.

SELAH: Don't mean it's true.

TIRASOL: Gotta mean somethin.

(Beat.)

SELAH: People talk.

TIRASOL: They talk all right.

SELAH: Talk until their tongues turn blue. Got *nothing* to do.

(Beans falling into bowl. Pause.)

TIRASOL: What's she gonna do?

MIRANDA: Who?

TIRASOL:

> Simone. What's she gonna do?
>
> *Got* to do somethin. Ain't she?
>
> Can't keep grievin forever.
>
> Ain't do a soul no good to *keep on* grievin.
>
> Bring nothin but chaos and misery on a person to do that.
>
> … What's she gonna do?

> *(Beat.)*

CAROLINE: Nothin.

TIRASOL: What you say?

CAROLINE: Nothin, I 'xpect.

TIRASOL. Nothin?

CAROLINE: Uh-huh.

TIRASOL: What you mean, "Nothin?" There ain't no such thing.

CAROLINE: Is too.

TIRASOL: What? What you gonna tell me is, "Nothin?" Huh?

SELAH: …Goin on. Lettin yourself just *go on.* That's a kind of nothin.

> *(To Caroline)* Eh?

CAROLINE: Uh-huh.

(Beat.)

TIRASOL: Bull. Throwing me bull, that's all you're doin.

    That woman's *got* to do somethin… Ain't been married a month.

SELAH: Mercy on the child.

CAROLINE: Have mercy.

MIRANDA: What's she gonna do?

(Pause.)

TIRASOL: Heard say she wrote a letter to the guvment.

MIRANDA: Did what?

TIRASOL: Wrote a letter. Cussed them out.

MIRANDA: That true?

TIRASOL: Yeh.

SELAH: Bull.

MIRANDA: What'd she day?

TIRASOL: Huh?

MIRANDA: What'd she say in this letter?

TIRASOL: She say all sorts of things. Tell guvment this, that…Cussed them right
out.

MIRANDA: Yeh?

TIRASOL: That's what they say.

MIRANDA: That's somethin.

TIRASOL: That's somethin all right.

MIRANDA: …Grand.

TIRASOL: Eh?

MIRANDA: To write somethin like that? To the guvment? Grand, I say. Grand and
valiant.

TIRASOL: Grand?

MIRANDA: Why, just the notion of it is… I couldn't do it. It may be a small measure
of

significance, but writing down a letter *is* somethin.

SELAH: …Mercy on the child.

CAROLINE: Have mercy.

(Pause.)

TIRASOL: Got a right.

MIRANDA: Course she does.

CAROLINE: What you say?

TIRASOL: You cuss guvment out like that, it's a right.

CAROLINE: Got *no* right.

TIRASOL: What you say now?

CAROLINE: Ain't guvment's fault. People die in wars all the time. She ain't the
only one.

SELAH: That's right.

(Beat.)

CAROLINE: Your man, he passed on, didn't he?

SELAH: In the second war.

CAROLINE: …The second war.

SELAH:

> Sweet boy he was, too. Never bring me no harm.
>
> Not like the other so-called men in my life.
>
> No, that boy was as good as can be.
>
> Hungry, is all. Hungry for war. Couldn't wait to be part of it.
>
> Wanted the test of battle more than anythin else, that boy.
>
> Wanted it more than lovin,
>
> more than any kind of lovin a woman could give him.
>
> I'd sit up at night and think, That boy is a fool.
>
> What's he doin thinkin about war when he's got me
>
> ready to walk hot coals for him if I had to? What's he thinking?
>
> But he didn't know no better. He was young. Young and hungry.
>
> A thirst for war is simply too much for a young man.
>
> It's a kind of call: a call to desperate livin.
>
> Boys listen to it, their ears aflame:
>
> Oh when the rapture of war comes upon them unbelievable in its truth.

Just didn't know no better.

…Sweet boy. Sweet sweet boy.

CAROLINE: And he died.

SELAH: Yeh, he died. Fell out of a plane and into the sky, body on fire. I don't think he ever saw the ground.

CAROLINE: And you ain't wrote the guvment.

SELAH: No sir.

CAROLINE: It was your cross.

SELAH: Mine to bear.

CAROLINE: You just moved on.

SELAH: Had to. Couldn't write.

Couldn't write, couldn't read. Not at the time.

CAROLINE: You just moved on.

SELAH: Yeah

(Pause.)

TIRASOL: He was a stupid boy.

CAROLINE: Who?

TIRASOL: Jamie.

MIRANDA: Was not.

TIRASOL: Stupid. Didn't know anythin, that boy: always walkin around, not a thought in his brain.

SELAH: She loved him.

CAROLINE: Yeh, she did.

SELAH: He loved her.

MIRANDA: I don't know about that.

CAROLINE: You say he didn't?

TIRASOL: I say he was stupid. I don't think he knew what love was, 'cept for puttin his thing between a woman's legs.

MIRANDA: He could do that.

(Beat.)

CAROLINE: Oh, child. You just run wild. Got no mind at all.

MIRANDA: Ain't married him. Got some mind to do that.

TIRASOL: Sleepin with the devil, sleepin in the devil's bed.

SELAH: Mercy.

CAROLINE: Mercy on the child.

MIRANDA: It's war. Wartime makes you wild.

(Pause.)

TIRASOL: Say, you know where was that war?

MIRANDA: Which war?

TIRASOL: This war.

MIRANDA: Don't know. Some country, I 'xpect.

TIRASOL: …China?

MIRANDA:

> No, China's at that bottom of the ground,
>
> clear way to the other side of the earth,
>
> you gotta dig to find it. Not China.

CAROLINE: I used to know where it was.

TIRASOL: Yeh?

CAROLINE: Used to know 'xactly where it was. Can't remember the name.

> How come names do that?

MIRANDA: Do what?

CAROLINE: Escape us?

TIRASOL: Too many countries.

SELAH: Too many wars.

(Beat.)

TIRASOL: What's she doin now, I wonder?

CAROLINE: Don't now. Don't know nothin no more…

TIRASOL: She could go crazy, what all the talk goin round. Could go mad.

CAROLINE: She keep thinkin about him, yeh. She don't…

SELAH: I 'xpect she's sleepin. Gotta sleep off your mournin.

TIRASOL: Sleepin. Yeh. She could be doin that.

MIRANDA: I 'xpect she's dreamin.

TIRASOL: Dreamin? What she gonna be dreamin about with her grievin? She got no cause to dream.

MIRANDA: She got cause.

TIRASOL: Yeh?

MIRANDA: She's dreamin.

TIRASOL: What's she dreamin about?

MIRANDA: She's dreamin about his sweet eyes lookin at her… his tongue, his mouth…dreamin.

CAROLINE: You need some water, child. Gotta cool yourself off.

MIRANDA: It's hot.

CAROLINE: No excuse for talk like that. That's a dead-man you're talkin about.

        Gotta respect the dead same as the livin.

MIRANDA: Ain't said nothin.

CAROLINE:

    Said plenty, that mouth of yours.

    You got no right to talk about that man, especially not about his body.

    The man is dead. His body is in the ground.

    Ain't no dreamin of any kind about a dead-man's body,

    especially not when he's left a widow to remember him by.

MIRANDA: You sayin she ain't dreamin?

CAROLINE:

    I'm sayin: you gotta conduct yourself, no matter how much you ache for him.

(Beat.)

TIRASOL: Hot.

CAROLINE: Yeh.

MIRANDA: And she's dreamin…

CAROLINE: Mercy.

SELAH: Mercy on the child.

(Light change.)

3.

Apparition

Sound: slightly distorted helicopter flying overhead. Sound swells. Jamie appears. His clothes are rumpled, distressed, but he is physically intact.

JAMIE:

Oh—

I got beat up bad.

Those bullets went right through me.

Got holes all over: arms, chest, thigh…

Even my damn breathin's screwed up.

(Breathes audibly.) Hear that?

She was so sad when I left.

I was goin out on that bus to here,

and she just kept lookin at me. Like I did somethin.

What the hell is she sad about? I thought,

I'm the one who's leavin. I'm the one goin God knows where

to get God knows beat up so bad I can't even breathe.

But she just kept standin there on the side of the road,

the bus drivin off and all I could see was her

standin there on the side of the road with those eyes…

and then nothin.

'Cept for this picture.

And she don't even look that good in it:

her mouth's all crooked, eyes kind cross-eyed—

She don't look good at all.

(He tears the picture. Beat.)

Dear Simone…

I am beat up.

I am beat up bad.

4

Afternoon. Selah is hunting for stones in the ground. As she finds one to her liking,

she picks it up, and stores it in a small pouch she carries. Miranda runs in.

MIRANDA: I've heard say there are ghosts walkin the earth. Is it true?

SELAH: Course it's true. There are spirits 'round us all the time.

MIRANDA: Yeh?

SELAH: Uh-huh.

MIRANDA: Then how come we don't see them?

SELAH: 'Cause we feel them, that's why. Don't you feel them?

MIRANDA: I don't know.

SELAH:

> You got to know.
>
> Why, don't you sometimes walk 'round,
>
> and feel like there's someone walkin 'round with you,
>
> 'cept you can't see him?

MIRANDA: Guess so.

SELAH:

> I do. Not all the time, mind you, but sometimes…
>
> Oh, there is a powerful feelin I get
>
> that there's someone right here beside me. A strong, palpable feelin.

MIRANDA: Like a ghost?

SELAH: Yeh. You could call it that: a spirit, presence of some kind—walkin the earth

with me.

MIRANDA: Must feel scary.

SELAH: No. Feels nice. Like I'm protected.

MIRANDA: Protected?

SELAH:

That I'm not alone, not completely, no matter what I do.

Course, sometimes a bad sprit comes to haunt you,

and that can get scary all right.

Ain't no way that feels nice.

Why, one time a bad spirit got a hold of me,

and it took heaven and earth to rid myself of it. Heaven and earth…

Stubborn spirit, it was. Stubborn and nasty.

MIRANDA: Devil spirit?

SELAH:

Ain't so much the devil, as a meanness that come over me.

It's when it's mean that it's that worse kind of hauntin.

The world's mean enough already—

to have a mean spirit dome along and visit you:

well… ain't no place for it. No place at all.

MIRANDA: What'd you do?

SELAH: Hmm?

MIRANDA: Mean spirit. What'd you do?

SELAH:

    Got myself rid of it. You *got* to with bad spirits,

    otherwise they never stop hauntin you.

    Ol Lucy Hawkins's cousin, Aster Dean:

    she let a bad spirit into her, paid it no mind at all,

    figurin it'd let go of her when it done what it had to do;

    The woman turned right into a spook before our very eyes:

    grown her hair down to the ground white as ash,

    speakin in all kinds of tongue,

    lettin the meanness rise up out of her like untamed lava.

MIRANDA: Yeh? Bad spirit, huh?

SELAH: Untended.

MIRANDA: …Where's she now?

SELAH:

    Aster Dean? Don't know.

    I stopped speakin to her. We all did.

    Woman turns into a spook, can't keep socializin with her.

    Figure she must be off somewhere.

    In her state, it's better if she be off somewhere…

    (Beat.)

MIRANDA: And now?

SELAH: Eh, child?

MIRANDA: Right now. Is there a spirit here?

SELAH: …Yeh.

MIRANDA: Yeh?

SELAH: Course.

MIRANDA: How do you know?

SELAH: Just a feelin I get. Why are you so worried, child? You come upon a ghost

    today?

MIRANDA: I don't know.

SELAH: You know if you come upon one.

MIRANDA: …No.

SELAH: Then why the worry? You sick, child?

MIRANDA: No.

SELAH: Then what is it, then?

MIRANDA: Been thinkin about Simone and Jamie, is all. Thinkin bout her thinkin

bout

    him…

SELAH: You feel him?

MIRANDA: Huh?

SELAH: Feel his presence?

MIRANDA: Feel somethin. But it ain't him.

SELAH: How do you know if ain't him

MIRANDA: 'Cause it ain't. Why would I feel anythin?

SELAH: You slept with the man.

MIRANDA: So? That don't mean *nothin.*

Why, he wadn't even married then.

SELAH: Still slept with the man, shared in his spirit—

MIRANDA: No. Don't mean nothin! Don't mean I gotta believe in ghosts.

SELAH:

Oh, but you do.

If you don't, life just ain't the same. Ain't the same at all.

It'd be like goin 'round seein things one-half, instead of whole.

Don't you know it's up to the livin to recall the dead?

The one obligation we got besides bein born and dyin

is to recall those who have passed on to another life,

to signify their very physical passin.

It is our recallin that keeps spirits alive.

Now, I'm not sayin it's got to be Jamie.

You don't even have to know who it is you're recallin.

Why, there are ghosts who have been walkin this earth

for hundreds of years.

Old, tired ghosts who sit, and watch, and murmur.

Don't you ever feel that? The earth murmurin?

At night. When the world's asleep,

when you're lyin in bed before sleep overcomes you,

and all the sounds of the surroundin world

float in and around where you lay:

cars passin, off, down the road,

their tires squealin and hissin in the darkness;

the cracklin of leaves as they fall off the branch into the air,

their landings broken by hard ground;

split-splat of stones ripplin on water

before the whoosh of the night current takes them under.

Sounds. Floatin in and around,

until the space between you and slumber comes upon silence,

a silence that's so alive, so full of pulse and vibration,

you can hear them murmur: the ghosts of the earth.

'Tis not cause to be a-feared, child.

You got to take comfort in the murmurin,

for spirits wake to rumors of beauty and violence

to shiver our souls and remind us of our mortality.

'Tis not cause to be a-feared.

(Selah pulls out a bone necklace from her pouch, holds it out in front of Miranda.)

Come here. Let's see how this looks on you.

(Miranda turns away.)

It's all right to wander in your mind.

You got to wander before you can come to believe somethin.

That's why they say it like that: "Comin to believe."

It don't just happen. No sir.

You got to find your way to it, whatever it is,

whatever you set down and say you're goin to believe—

you got to find yourself to.

(Selah places necklace on Miranda.)

MIRANDA: I know one thing.

SELAH: Yeh? What would that be?

MIRANDA: I know I ain't loved Jamie. Not like Simone does.

SELAH: That's why he married her, child. That's why he married her.

(Light shift.)

5.

Simone walks in. There are traces of mud on her hands and dress.

SIMONE:

Truth is, I married him.

When you come right down to it,

I'm the one who did the marryin.

Jamie just fell into it.

In fact, I'd say we sort of fell into each other:

He didn't know what he was doin,

and I was still burnin with the memory of havin made love in his car.

It's a strange thing: desire.

It makes you do things for no other reason

than a mighty feelin you can't even put your finger on

says you *got* o do it…Strange.

Haven't cleaned up the house yet. Haven't even been in the house,

not for more than an hour or two at a time,

not since the wake.

I don't wanna go in there. It still smells like fried chicken.

And what stuff he had is in there, too.

It's too pitiful to sit around, touch it…wouldn't' know what to do…

I sleep in the yard.

It's been so hot, the cool nights feel good against my skin.

I like being next to the earth, right up against it,

lettin the moss tickle my belly and my toes,

Have it lick at me feel like a strange animal.

Feels good sinkin into the moist earth unencumbered.

Gives a sense of peace to things, kind of peace can't feel nowhere else.

Some nights I pretend I'm dead:

that I'm just a body restin on a piece of burial ground somewhere,

waitin for the heavens to take my soul away—

like those bodies you see lyin about sometimes,

people you ain't ever met, never seen even,

forgotten bodies that somehow are at peace on the ground

indebted to the cruelty of nature—

that's what I pretend.

It's gotten to where I can hold my breath for a minute

…sometimes two.

I lie on the cool ground, motionless, holdin my breath—

hush—

In hope that no one will find me,

that I will simply be lost forever, gone from this world.

But then a sound or a light in the sky will stir me,

and I am no longer at rest on a burial ground

but lyin all too awake in my yard,

sleepless, stirrin,

eyes that had been dream-less suddenly wide in motion,

searchin for the first signs of light.

I stay there. Eyes open. Starin at nothingness.

Until, sure enough, I see the hard sparkle of the sun

hit the edge of the fence, bounce against Lucy Hawkins window-pane,

and cut across my eyelids—close, hot.

I get up. I go into the house. I take off my clothes.

I pour myself a tall, very tall, glass of mint julep ice tea

with too much ice,

and when I finish the glass,

just as it is beginning to cool itself right through me—

the stench, the wretched stench of the chicken,

and of the candy-sweet perfumes Caroline and Selah wore that day,

sends me back outside:

where I throw on an old dress that's been hangin on the line too long

over my body

and take off

down to the water.

down to the water… and go fishin.

6

By the water. Simone is fishing. Miranda walks in.

MIRANDA: Ain't caught anythin yet?

SIMONE: Not yet.

MIRANDA: Gotta be patient. Gotta wait.

SIMONE: Mmm-hmm.

MIRANDA: I used to go fishin, so I know.

SIMONE: Yeh?

MIRANDA: Never actually fished myself, mind you/

SIMONE: Huh?

MIRANDA: My Granny'd take me. When I was little.

> She's the one who did the actual fishin.

> I'd just watch her. *(Pulls out a cigarette)* Smoke?

SIMONE: No.

MIRANDA: Yeh, she'd take me. I didn't know what was goin on. I used to say,

> "Grammy, what's this? Grammy, what's that?" "Hush, child," she'd say,

"Hush."

> *(Miranda lights cigarette, smokes.)*

SIMONE: *(To herself):* Hush…

MIRANDA: Swear. I don't know how she put up with me, but she did.

33

She'd just smile…sit there…fish.

She'd smoke, too.

Not cigarettes, but a big ol' cigar 'bout this thick.

You should've seen the smoke she'd blow out of that thing.

Swirls and swirls of it. Like chimney smoke.

And it smelled too.

Not sweet like Caroline's perfume. But strong. Like dust and ginger.

SIMONE: Yeh?

MIRANDA:

Used to make them herself, the cigars.

Grow the tobacco out back,

roll the leaves up in the finest paper,

suck on it til one end'd be completely wet with saliva and juice,

and then she'd light up, the raw tobacco just envelopin the air.

Oh, and she'd smile…she'd smile the biggest grin…

Teeth turned black, she'd still smile.

I hated it. All of it. The cigars. Everything.

Felt like it was punishment every time I had to go out with her.

Grammy and her goddamn tobacco.

But after a while, I don't know how it occurred,

the smell of that tobacco became like heaven itself.

"When we goin fishin, Grammy? When we going?"

"Patience, child. Patience." And she'd smile, gather her gear, and take me down to the water.

The sun'd be comin up. You could see the rays just peerin.

Flashes of light bouncing off the water blindin you

as you looked into the mornin haze.

And she'd smile, lay out the tobacco, and start rollin them cigars,

her hands movin sharp and quick

like one of those gunfighters on TV, all eyes and trigger fingers,

rollin and lightin up. Smokin and castin a line.

It was all of a piece with Grammy.

I'd sit there, wallowin in the smell,

swear all the angels had come down to pay us a visit.

Used to try to catch the rings of smoke in my mouth,

like some sort of weird human kind of fish.

I must've caught a hundred rings one time. One hundred.

I swear it, it was the best part of goin fishin.

In fact, for the longest time, that's what I thought fishin was:

just somethin you did to go smokin.

SIMONE: Would she catch anythin?

MIRANDA:

Every once in a while, sure.

Caught a yellow perch once—gutted it, chopped it up, ate it for supper.

But I can't say I remember her actually catchin

much of anythin in particular.

Not like you see in those pictures they got all over the walls at the diner

of people standing tall next to their big fish and smilin.

Can't say she ever got took a picture like that.

… Got somethin?

SIMONE: Feels like somethin's on the line.

MIRANDA: Maybe you got somethin.

SIMONE: …It's gone.

MIRANDA:

That happens. Used to happen to Grammy all the time.

Just when she'd think a fish would bite, it'd go away.

They're not as stupid as we think—fish.

I mean, if I were a fish, I wouldn't want to be somebody's supper.

I'd know better than to jump at the first thing I saw.

…What you thinkin?

SIMONE: Hmm?

MIRANDA: Hmm? What you thinkin?

SIMONE: Nothin.

MIRANDA: Awful quiet. Gotta be thinkin 'bout somethin.

SIMONE: Just thinkin.

MIRANDA: What about?

SIMONE: Thinkin 'bout the world.

MIRANDA: The world? What you thinkin bout the world?

SIMONE: Thinkin that it's some place, y'know.

That it's such a big place, and all these things happen—

wars, fires, hurricanes, sickness—

I think, How come the soil don't just *burst?*

How come it don't just burst from all this excitement?

I know I would.

If it were me, I'd *explode* in a thousand little pieces,

scatter myself in bits all over the earth—

wars, fires, hurricanes comin up out of me

in *bile* colored gray, scarlet and indigo.

Come up and out of me till there'd be *nothin,*

just open space: a whole other world.

I don't know how the soil can take it. I really don't.

(Beat.)

MIRANDA·

Selah says the soil's stronger than all of us,

on account of that's where we go once we pass on.

…And that's where we get our strength, too, from the soil.

SIMONE: Yeh?

MIRANDA: That's what she says.

SIMONE: How you get strength from somethin that's torn apart, *busted* open?

How you get it then?

MIRANDA: …Maybe a different soil come up.

SIMONE: Huh?

MIRANDA: A different soil, a different earth underneath the old one.

>   Maybe it'd come up and…I don't know, it'd do somethin.

SIMONE: …Damn.

MIRANDA: Fish ain't jumpin for nothin, huh? They'll come 'round.

>   Grammy'd sometimes have to wait two, three hours before a fish'd jump.

>   That's when she really put her time in smokin.

>   You sure you don't want one? It's good.

SIMONE: I know.

>   *(Beat.)*

MIRANDA: So, what you do, you clean the house yet?

SIMONE: No.

MIRANDA: Gotta clean it.

SIMONE: Ain't gotta *do* nothin.

MIRANDA: Selah says you don't clean a house after someone's—

SIMONE: Hell what Selah says! I ain't doin it. I ain't goin in there.

MIRANDA:

>   Well, she says if you don't clean it, you collect bad spirits.

>   Wan then you can' even go into the house. Even if you want to.

>   Gotta BURN IT DOWN. 'Cause fire's the only thing

that'll scare bad spirits off for good.

SIMONE: She say that?

MIRANDA:

Yeh. And she said you don't get rid of bad spirits,

They come 'round and turn on you—turn you into a *spook.*

SIMONE: I ain't a spook.

MIRANDA: That's what she said.

SIMONE: Well, I ain't! Hell, who wants to be that?

Nobody talkin to you, nobody lookin at you—nobody wants that.

MIRANDA: …So, you gonna clean it? Huh?

SIMONE: Gonna do somethin.

MIRANDA: Yeh? What you gonna do?

SIMONE: Gonna keep myself far away from it. As far from the house as…

Just stay close to the water. Maybe I can lose myself in it.

Lose myself…That'd be somethin.

7.

Evening. Caroline is wringing items of wet clothing into a tin washtub. She sings to
herself.

CAROLINE:

Take me to the flood, Lilah.

Take me to the flood.

I wanna see the moon winkin

through river of blood

through river of blood.

Take me in a boar, Lilah.

Take me in a boat.

And there I'll see the night tumble

as weary stars float,

as they float.

Wash away my trouble.

Hmm-mmm.

Send me along.

Steal away my sorrow.

Under and gone.

Take me in a flood, Lilah.

Take me in a flood.

And there I'll see the boat sinkin

through ocean of mud.

8.

Visitation

By the water. Night. Ella Fitzgerald's recording of Van Heusen and Burke's song
"Moonlight Becomes You" is heard. Simone is listening to a transistor radio.
Drinking whiskey from the bottle, and swaying to the music. Song plays. Starts to fade
in, out, as it is interrupted by static. Simone changes the station. More static.
Changes back. Song is heard for a moment, then disappears in static. Simone turns
off the radio. Jamie appears.

JAMIE: It's the radio.

(Simone sees him. He does not see her.)

Damn radio's no good. I had me a radio like that once.

Transistor radio? Yeh. Piece of shit.

Only thing it was good for was a bit of rock 'n' roll.

And they only played that at night.

It was hard to listen to 'cause the music was loud,

but the radio had to be kept quiet.

And you know how the volume is on these things—it's either *up* or down.

Yeh. It's the radio.

Wasn't the song. No. Song went good. Fit the moon just right.

If it wadn't for the radio, it just might've been perfect.

(Simone circles him slowly.)

Sure don't get those too often. A moment perfect in time?

I don't think I've ever had one.

Maybe the day I was married. And then not even the whole day even.

Just that moment when I looked at her. Right before the vows.

Before the words "I do" could even make their way our of my throat.

Just that moment. Closest I ever come to perfect.

And it ain't had nothin to do with sex.

Not that I haven't had it good.

Guys in my unit? They're amazed at the number of chicks I've had.

Simply amazed.

But it still ain't got me to perfect.

Hell, you grow up thinkin your whole life sex is the only way

you can get to perfect, but then when your life happens,

somethin else happens.

Ain't nobody tell you about desire. It just come upon you.

Like somethin that ain't even real.

Like it come down from someplace in the ether. Down and through you...

And it ain't about your dick or…It's just a look.

Or the way her hair falls in front of her face, or…

Closest I ever come.

(Simone is very close to him now. He moves away.)

Hot ain't it? Damn near burnin up.

Done nothin but run around all night lookin for my arm

got shot off someplace. Thought if I looked for it, I'd find it.

Don't know how many times I come across part of somebody,

A piece of 'im that's found its way to another part of the land.

Why, I found a whole hand once.

Belonged to some guy named Toomy. Not a bad guy. Just stupid.

I recognized it right away 'cause he had this tattoo on his hand,

somethin like a crossbow and a dragon's tail with flames all around it,

I saw it and I said, "Man, this is Toomy. This is Toomy's hand.

And it was clear way 'cross someplace else, miles from the rest of 'im

Just layin' there. With no one to claim it.

Course, I picked it up. Only fair thing to do.

Carried it in my pocket for a while.

Then I just threw it away.

I mean, the man was stupid. Got his fuckin hand shot off.

I didn't want Toomy's slow-trigger curse on me, y'know what I'm sayin?

Look and look. Ain't seen my arm nowhere.

Thirsty, too. Throat's all…

(She holds out the whiskey bottle. He grabs it. It is as if the bottle has simply appeared before him.)

Yeh. *(He drinks.)* Yeah.

Now, you see? This is good shit. That is real good shit.

This is the kind of shit that's gonna find me my arm.

Puts me in mind of my girl. My girl, she always got the best whiskey.

One night in the car, we went off and parked up by ol man Hawkins's mill,

and she pulled out this *absolute goddamn kick-ass* whiskey

that just about set my tongue on fire.

Swear. Everywhere I look now, I see fire.

Nothin but red air splittin itself all around me,

The sky electric with blood and flame.

It's the killin. It puts you in shame.

Poppin bodies, takin 'em down—takes you down with it.

Got no way to cool yourself off. Not deep inside.

You're like tinder: tremble and spark. All the time.

Tremble, and…

(She reaches toward him. He walks away.)

Whiskey's startin to hit. Swear, it's got the best kick, whiskey does.

(Looking out) What's that? That the hell is that?

It was like a flare in the sky. Blue-orange.

Off. Behind the stars. See it?

Thought I saw it.

Water sure is still. Storm must be comin.

Water gets still like that, somethin's gonna break.

Gotta keep lookin. Gotta keep movin.

Storm hits, I'll never find anythin. It'll all wash away for sure.

(He walks away. Is almost gone when:)

SIMONE: Jamie?

(He stops)

45

JAMIE: Hell of a storm. Hell of a storm come this way.

(He exits.)

SIMONE: Jamie!

(Blackout.)

9.

*Night. Tirasol holds a skein of yarn, which Caroline is unwinding and rolling into a
ball.*

TIRASOL: Must be up to somethin.

CAROLINE: Eh?

TIRASOL: No word? Sure sign a person's up to somethin ain't right.

CAROLINE: Leave her be.

TIRASOL: Can't. It's not in me.

CAROLINE: You know, I think Selah is right: you got *nothin* to do.

TIRASOL: Selah's the one who's got nothin.

CAROLINE: Oh yeh? Then how come you done nothin but spy on that poor woman
ever since his body done touch the ground?

TIRASOL: Ain't spyin.

CAROLINE: What you call it, then?

TIRASOL: Don't know.

CAROLINE: Now, that is bull. Clear as can be.

(Beat.)

TIRASOL:

> Don't like death. Can't stand to be around it.
>
> So many men died in this town, havin Jamie catch his like that
>
> makes me feel rotten.
>
> I go about my business, yeh, but the air's thick with grievin.
>
> Don't have to look close, but you can see the phantoms
>
> sure take shape as the mist comes up on the water:
>
> strange, throttled phantoms jostlin the livin flesh.
>
> Makes me feel hard inside. Like my guts are all twisted.
>
> Don't like bein part of shame. And that's what it is—a land of murder:
>
> bones of the dead suffocatin the earth one war upon the other,
>
> howls of widows ensnared in the wind
>
> crumplin 'gainst the skin of the water
>
> and us, sittin here, goin on.
>
> Well, don't like bein here. And goin on, bein here.
>
> Makes me feel burdened.
>
> To think of her still thinkin of him, and not a word at that...

Can't stand it.

CAROLINE: Don't you miss him, though?

TIRASOL: Jamie?

CAROLINE: Yeh.

TIRASOL: Only as someone who used to be but now isn't.

CAROLINE: I do.

TIRASOL: Yeh?

CAROLINE:

He wadn't no saint,

and I never really took to him like other women did.

But now that I actually think of him,

now that he's in the ground

and his soul is hoverin over the trees and water lookin for mercy,

I think, He had a true expression. A kind of honesty.

I miss that.

TIRASOL: *(To herself):* Yeh.

10.

Woods. Night. Simone runs in.

SIMONE: Don't run off on me.

You move so fast I can barely catch you.

Where'd you learn to move like that? Huh?

You're like lightnin. Just skimmin the surface of the air.

And where is it you run to? Huh?

What the hell are you lookin for?

There's nothin. Nothin here.

Just tree, and water and goddamn branches that got me all cut up.

And all you think about is runnin.

Like the air's gonna take you someplace you've never been.

Well, I can't lose you—can't let myself lose…

I heard you. I know I did.

I saw you. I know. –I did.

You have you come back to lose you—

You tell me you're here. You tell me.

You ain't goddamn leavin me again.

I am gonna find the breath.

I'm gonna trespass on the night.

I'm gonna swallow the stars until I find you.

'Cause I am comin to you—yeh—

don't know where I'll find you, but I can feel you in my skin—

oh—like tinder.

11.

Woods. Night. Miranda walks in with a jar of fireflies in her hand.

MIRANDA: *(As an incantation):*

A hundred and one fireflies in my jar,

Light my way, near and far.

If I catch them, will you say—

JAMIE: *(Appearing):* What you got there? In that jar?

MIRANDA: …Fireflies. Can't see my way round her without them. Not this time of

night.

JAMIE: Dark, huh?

MIRANDA: Don't seem dark to you?

JAMIE: I'm kinda…used to it.

MIRANDA: You mean to tell me you can find you way 'round here

without even so much as a firefly to guide you?

JAMIE: Can—do it.

MIRANDA: You must be from real far, 'cause I ain't met nobody

who can see in the dark like that.

I bet you're from one of those places with wide water.

JAMIE: *(To himself):* Wide water…

MIRANDA: From one of those places where you can roam 'round.

JAMIE: ...Wouldn't mind—that.

MIRANDA: What's it like?

JAMIE: Huh?

MIRANDA: Roamin?

JAMIE: It's long. Days—long. Nights, too. Can't get no rest.

> Just go 'round 'n' 'round on some road ain't got. —Can't stop.

> Somethin inside—won't let—

> *(Indicating fireflies)* They're gonna die all bunched up like that.

MIRANDA: Won't.

JAMIE: They're climbin jar like mad. Can't breathe—there.

MIRANDA: They breathe fine.

JAMIE: They'll die.

MIRANDA: What are you worried about? They're just fireflies.

JAMIE: Seen too much death where I've been. Let them go now. Let them go.

MIRANDA: If I do that, I won't be able to see anythin.

JAMIE: What you gonna see this time of night? What you wanna see?

MIRANDA: I want to see a ghost!

> Selah says, "Ghost rise up out of the water, and go in among the trees."

> I've been aimin to see one. For some time now. Ain't gonna stop.

> Ain't gonna deprive myself of a real-live vision,

> just 'cause some stupid fireflies are bunched up in a jar.

JAMIE: Let—them—go.

MIRANDA: You want 'em? Is that it? You want the goddamn fireflies? Here. Take

them.

(She exits. Beat. He opens the jar.)

JAMIE: …Go.

(Fireflies rise up out of the jar and into the night.)

12.

Morning. Tirasol and Caroline are slicing squash.

TIRASOL: Vanished.

CAROLINE: Hmm?

TIRASOL: Out-right vanished.

CAROLINE: She ain't vanished.

TIRASOL: Ain't been heard from all night. Might as well be.

CAROLINE: Maybe she's wanderin.

TIRASOL: All night and straight to the morning?

CAROLINE: Could be.

(Beat.)

TIRASOL: What's she doin?

CAROLINE: Huh?

TIRASOL: Can't just wander for the sake of wanderin. Gotta be a purpose to it.

> And if there ain't no purpose, then…what's she doin?

> What's she doing wanderin with no shoes on all night, all mornin?

> What's she doin?

> I think she's vanished. It's simply too long a time without word.

CAROLINE: You worry too much.

TIRASOL: Don't it bother you?

CAROLINE: Of course. But I don't go round thinkin about it. I can't live that way.

> Can you imagine if I went 'round thinkin 'bout every little thing?

> I wouldn't get out of bed in the morning. My head'd be heavy.

> Weighed down with thought. Wouldn't know what to do first.

> And things gotta get done. Now matter what goes 'round.

> Sure, I worry. I just don't let the worryin occupy me, that's all.

> Like Selah says, "Got to move on."

TIRASOL: Gotta do somethin.

CAROLINE: Can't you give the woman peace?

TIRASOL: No. Not when her house is sittin there with its smell and his stuff.

> Can't give her *no* peace.

> Why, don't nobody want to go near it no more.

> Turnin itself into a spook house, it is.

CAROLINE: Just 'cause she's been gone all night don't mean it's come to that.

TIRASOL: How you know? You heard somethin?

CAROLINE: No.

TIRASOL: Then how you know?

CAROLINE: I just know we got to give it time.

TIRASOL: Why? What do we got to wait for?

> We wait for ten thousand crows to come down
>
> and start peckin at the house gashin blood from the sky?
>
> That what we wait for? And how long do we wait? Five, ten days? Years?
>
> How long do we wait before we just *do* somethin 'bout it? Huh?
>
> How long?

(Caroline stops slicing squash.)

CAROLINE: Swear. You've been up too long, y'know that.

> You ain't even thinkin what you're sayin.
>
> You wanna *clean house* before you even know what kind of spirit's in there?
>
> You wanna mess around when you've not even sure if Simone's out wanderin,

or   vanished, or somewhere in the belly of the house

> lost in the chicken slime and darkness?
>
> You thinkin 'bout anythin' 'cept your own burden?
>
> You thinkin' 'bout anythin at all?
>
> Or do you just wanna toy with the spirits?

Play your worryin, see if heaven and earth come down?

You need to sleep a while. Rest your head. Give it time.

Believe me, time come. And when it does—we'll do somethin.

13.

Specter

Jamie is caught in a flash of unnatural light.

JAMIE: What I?—

Can't remember

Can't remem—you

Simone!

(Simone appears. She wears a dress of chicken bones and scarlet ribbons. A
handprint of blood across her face.)

SIMONE: I am right here. See?

JAMIE:

Brain is

SIMONE:

fragments. Yes

JAMIE:

Like fragments

fallen

SIMONE: falling

JAMIE: chunks—memory

SIMONE:

      pieces

      falling

JAMIE:

      Takin me down

SIMONE:

      Take me.

      Take me.

JAMIE:

      Down

SIMONE:

      Take me.

JAMIE:

      Past light

SIMONE:

      Sky

JAMIE:

      Shadow

SIMONE:

      Stirs me

SIMONE AND JAMIE:

> into somethin

> I don't understand

JAMIE:

> Not

SIMONE AND JAMIE:

> face

JAMIE:

> name.

SIMONE AND JAMIE:

> Lost.

> Can't remember.

> *(Beat.)*

JAMIE:

> Road has unwound.

SIMONE:

> Hot

> burning.

JAMIE:

> I am in

> fever,

SIMONE:

    Take me.

JAMIE:

    Fever.

SIMONE:

    Now!

    Take me.

    Take me.

    (Beat.)

JAMIE:

    Peckin

SIMONE:

    no.

JAMIE:

    Lone bird peckin.

SIMONE:

    no peace—no.

JAMIE:

    Clawin at

SIMONE AND JAMIE:

    skin.

JAMIE:

>Rippin

SIMONE AND JAMIE:

>vein.

JAMIE:

>Tearin past.

SIMONE AND JAMIE

>blood,

>bone.

(Jamie and Simone emit a long, silent cry. Beat.)

JAMIE:

>Hot.

>Sun. Silence.

>Hope—wind—

SIMONE:

>Jamie?

JAMIE:

>comes.

>Or I'll burn. I will.

>I am burning.

SIMONE:

Can you see me?

JAMIE:

Like one of those Red Demon firecrackers I used to get when I was a kid.

SIMONE:

Can you see me now?

JAMIE:

True devil...

SIMONE:

See.

See.

See.

See.

(She hits herself.)

See?!

(Silence. He looks at her.)

JAMIE:

Yes.

(He reaches out to her.)

Let—me—go.

(Simone lets out a sob. Blackout.

14.

Lights come up on Selah, Caroline, Tirasol and Miranda, brooms in hand. They
speak-sing the following "Spirit Call":

SELAH:

Spirit, you here?

CAROLINE:

Spirit, you here?

TIRASOL:

Get away, spirit.

MIRANDA:

Get away, spirit.

(They repeat the above lines. After a beat, they begin to sweep.)

CAROLINE:

Don't wanna take you up to heaven.

Don't wanna take you up, no sir.

Don't wanna send your soul a-temptin.

Don't wanna send your soul nowhere.

TIRASOL:

'Cause I'm gonna sweep you under my feet.

I'm gonna sweep you off this floor.

I'm gonna sweep you straight to the devil

Ain't gonna sin 'round this house no more.

SELAH:

Oh, Lord.

CAROLINE:

Father, can you hear me?

SELAII:

Oh, Lord.

ALL:

Hey. Uh.

SELAH:

Oh, Lord.

ALL:

Save this house from fallin.

SELAH AND CAROLINE:

Sprit, don't you come 'round this house now more.

CAROLINE:

Don't wanna let you ride to graceland.

Don't wanna let you ride, no sir.

'Cause if I lead you to the graceland,

I'll be in the devil's house for sure.

SELAH:

Oh, Lord.

CAROLINE:

Father, can you help me?

SELAH:

Oh, Lord.

Oh, Lord.

ALL:

Keep this house from fallin.

CAROLINE:

Spirit, don't you come 'round this house no more

TIRASOL:

'Cause I'm gonna sweep you off this floor now.

I'm gonna sweep you out of sight.

I'm gonna sweep you straight to hell now.

I'm gonna sweep you with all my might.

SELAH:

Oh, Lord.

ALL:

> Father, can you hear me?

SELAH:

> Oh, Lord.

ALL:

> Hey, Uh.

SELAH:

> Oh, Lord.

ALL:

> Save this house from fallin.
>
> Spirit, don't you come 'round this house no more.

TIRASOL:

> Spirit, don't you come 'round this house…

> *(Beat.)*

MIRANDA:

> Chili pepper
>
> cornbread
>
> ice water
>
> alligator
>
> Spirit, fly away.

(Beat.)

ALL:

Chili pepper

cornbread

ice water

alligator

Spirit, fly away.

SELAH:

Oh, Lord.

ALL:

Father, can you hear me?

SELAH:

Oh, Lord.

Oh, Lord.

ALL:

Save this house from fallin.

Spirit, don't you come 'round this house...

(They stop sweeping. Beat.)

CAROLINE:

Spirit, fly away.

Spirit, no more.

TIRASOL:

Spirit, fly away.

Spirit, no more.

MIRANDA:

Spirit, fly away.

Spirit…

SELAH:

…No more.

15.

In the background, a turquoise sky dotted with black crows. In the foreground is Simone before a garbage can. She is warning layers of Jamie's clothes.

SIMONE: You got to burn things. Got to burn 'em so they'll go away.

You don't burn 'em, they just stick around forever.

You burn things, they go away.

(She takes off one item of clothing, draws a lighter from her pocket, holds item out in front of her, burns it, throws it into garbage can. Small fire.)

They disappear down the path of nothingness

where fire and ash and air get all mixed up together

and turn into sky and breathin

That's what they tell me, anyway.

'Cept the more I burn things, the more they stay in my mind:

The blue shirt

he wore when we were out by the water,

the way he looked at me then, and took his hand

and ran it along inside me,

so a trickle of sweat stayed, restin, on his brow

wonderin where it was gonna go next;

(Throws shirt into fire) You burn things, they go away.

The shape of his torso

permanently outlined

in the small folds and crisp creases

of his grease-stained workshirt

fresh with the smell of gasoline and oil, and...

all the other mysteries of the garage;

(Throws shirt into the fire) You burn 'em, they go away.

The softness of his skin

in the white jersey

comin up behind me in the kitchen

while I was cookin the chicken fricassee,

and the steam was comin up out of the pot

and he was squeezing me firm, soft, in his white jersey—

jersey he wore with no underpants on,

so that the sweat and smell of his member

became a part of that jersey

as much as its frayed cotton fibers and green number 21;

(She throws the jersey into the fire.)

Things have a way of stayin in the mind.

No burnin can stop your mind from thinkin.

Only by losin yourself completely can you stop yourself from thinkin.

Either that, or by dyin.

Nobody knows for sure whether you keep thinkin once you're dead,

but I figure once you're gone from this world,

the things of this world can't be the same.

And that's got to be comfortin somehow.

To not think.

(To self) Burn things. Go away.

It's takin my self down that's hard.

Every time I try—

lettin the spark brush against my skin,

Holdin my breath

Til I feel myself drown in the gulf of fire—

the too-much-ness of this life calls to me

and brings me back from

Ash.

They're all of a piece now: blue, white, sweat, smells—

Locked in flame.

Burn things. Don't go away.

(She takes off the last layer of Jamie's clothing and throws it into garbage can.
She is left wearing a white cotton shift. Light change.)

16.

Lights come up on Selah. Tirasol and Miranda are lit softly in the space, surrounding
her.

SELAH: Lay the flowers out.

       Lay them on the hard floor.

       The dead-man has come by.

       Press the flowers into the cracks in the earth,

       flowers with veins of purple and green.

       Set them on the ground.

       Let the soil swallow them bloom to stem.

       Call the blues for the dead-man.

       For there's told a story

       about a ribbon of petals

       that wrapped itself in a garland

       'round the circumference of the world

       and called out:

ALL *(Sung)*:

       Ai-ah!

       La-le lai-ah!

       Ai-ah!

       La le lai!

SELAH *(Spoken)*: My feet will go on marching.

       The dead-man goes by.

17.

Chimera

Sound of a moving train. Jamie and Simone are on the train. Jamie is leaning against her. Train sound underscores the scene.

JAMIE: Simone?

SIMONE: Yes.

JAMIE: Where do you think everybody is?

SIMONE: What do you mean?

JAMIE: People. There's no people anywhere.

SIMONE: They're in their houses. Locked away.

Protectin themselves from the elements.

(Beat.)

JAMIE: Simone?

SIMONE: Yes.

JAMIE: Where will we end up, you think?

We'll have to jump off. We can't just keep goin.

SIMONE: I know.

(Beat.)

JAMIE: How'll we pick?

SIMONE: Hmm?

JAMIE: How'll we pick which one, which stop?

SIMONE: Jump off. We'll just jump off, see where we land.

(Train sound swells briefly.)

We're just whizzing, aren't we? Flyin through the night.

I like when it goes fast. Like that.

You feel like you're part of the train:

part of this big machinery that's cuttin through space and time

and all the crooked ways left in this earth.

It's like bein free for a second.

(Beat.)

JAMIE: Simone?

SIMONE: Hmm?

JAMIE: Sing me somethin.

SIMONE: What?

JAMIE: A song.

SIMONE: I don't remember the words to anythin.

JAMIE: Make 'em up. I don't care. Just sing to me.

Make me go to sleep.

(After a moment, she sings. Train sound fades out, as she does so.)

SIMONE:

Sleep on—rocky water.

Send my baby down.

Moon come up.

Turn the world 'round.

Sleep on—rocky water.

Thunder in a cloud.

Rest your heard upon me.

Hush now, child.

Lay your head upon me.

Hush…

(She stops singing. He has fallen asleep.)

It's quite possible we're made out of air.

That we're deep-down truly made of air.

That the rest is just stuff to keep us tied to the ground,

To keep us from flyin.

(Lights fade.)

18.

Miranda, Caroline, Tirasol and Selah are smoking cigars amidst a blanket of purple flowers.

MIRANDA: I'm wore out.

CAROLINE: Yeh.

MIRANDA: I'm plain wore out.

TIRASOL: Spirits are hard.

CAROLINE: Yeh. They're hard.

SELAH: Nobody said it'd be easy to get rid of a spirit.

MIRANDA: Smells nice, though.

CAROLINE: Flowers, yeh.

MIRANDA: Flowers and tobacco—their smells just comin up together.

CAROLINE: Rich.

MIRANDA: Yeh.

TIRASOL: Strong.

MIRANDA: Yeh. Like the whole world's gonna bust open with the smell.

SELAH: It's been a long time.

MIRANDA: Mmm?

SELAH: Long time since I swept a spirit up and out of here.

      Must've been…Some other war.

CAROLINE: …Another war.

SELAH: Why, I remember Lucy Hawkins, Caroline and I,

      we shouted so hard we couldn't speak for days and days

      after that sweepin. Lost our speech.

      (To Caroline) You remember that?

CAROLINE: I remember.

SELAH: It was hard, it was.

CAROLINE: Uh-huh.

SELAH: Getting' harder.

CAROLINE: Yeh.

MIRANDA: It's war.

SELAH: More than that.

MIRANDA: Huh?

SELAH: People don't know how to honor the land no more.

      Bad spirits been 'round all the time, sure,

      but these hard ones,

      that wear you down with hunger and anger,

      those come from a different soil,

      a soul that's been scarred, spat on, taken a killin.

      This land's become corrupt inside.

Damn wonder everyone's not wore out.

(Beat.)

MIRANDA: Still feels like somethin.

TIRASOL: What you talkin about?

MIRANDA: Don't know. Just feels like somethin's still here.

SELAH: It's the murmurin, child. That's what you feel

MIRANDA: Don't feel like murmurin. Feels more like—

SELAH: Ain't just about "feeling," child.

> Spirit is vision: fragment and memory reflected in the mind's eye.
>
> You got to see it. Inside you.
>
> It's in the heart where we see things.
>
> It's in the heart where we lay to rest trouble and joy.
>
> Go on, now. Let it come into you.

MIRANDA: …Don't see nothin.

SELAH: Look hard. Go on.

MIRANDA: …See somethin.

CAROLINE: Yeh?

SELAH: What'd you see, child?

MIRANDA: I see small lights walkin up and down the sky.

TIRASOL: Yeh?

MIRANDA: Catchin hold of the wind. And dancin.

CAROLINE: Mercy.

SELAH: Mercy on the child.

19.

In the background, a bone yard looking on to a wide sea. In the foreground is Simone.

She wars a pale green dress and is barefoot. Jamie's dog tags hang around her neck.

SIMONE: I got up this mornin and said to myself,

"I'm gonna find me some shoes.

I'm gonna find me some shoes

So I can walk this earth and see where my feet land.

See what my feet see that my head can't."

You need shoes

'cause bare you're just another part of the earth—

not on top of it, not above it—

ain't no way you can own a part of this world if you don't got shoes.

So, I set out. My toes wigglin.

I set out in search of what would find me.

Not long before walkin became too much.

I got on my knees,

rubbed my hands in the ground,

and said to myself, "Find them.

And if you don't find them—

Don't look back.

'Cause what is waitin for you

is the footprint of every other mad soul

who lost their wiggle on the search for a bit of stride."

And as I was rubbin, my hands raw with motion,

I found this spot, where there was nothin.

And in this spot, I found myself a piece of cardboard

that had belonged to a bucket of chicken.

I looked at it. Looked at it hard. Took my nose to it.

But it didn't smell no more.

Didn't smell like nothing 'cept the dirt it come from.

I thought, The underneath of the earth must be littered

for miles and miles with pieces of cardboard

from buckets of chicken that have been buried—cast off—

by those that have loved, lost or seen too much

of the earth's ways to believe in them.

(Reveals Kentucky Fried Chicken box "shoes" that have been off to one side,

unseen, and she sets them before her.)

I got off my knees.

And as I stood there,

somethin come over me:

and I just took a blade to it,

a sharp blade of grass,

and with it I cut myself some soles,

some soles to walk this earth,

and strapped them to my feet with a piece of chicken wire

till my feet bled—

bled,

but navigatin the world.

(Simone steps into her "shoes."

The sound of bagpipes—a hymn—is heard, as if from a distance. She

takes off the dog tags and sets them aside. She stands, looking out.

The bone yard slowly disappears, until all that can be see is a wide,

wide sea. The sound of bagpipes swells. Lights slowly fade.)

END OF PLAY

CARIDAD SVICH

Caridad Svich is a playwright-songwriter-translator and editor of Cuban-Spanish-Argentine-Croatian descent. She is the recipient of a Harvard University Radcliffe Institute for Advanced Study Bunting fellowship, a TCG/Pew National Theatre Artist Grant, and has been short-listed twice for the PEN USA-West Award in Drama. Her play with alt-country songs *Thrush* premiered at Salvage Vanguard Theatre in Austin in October 2006, and her adaptation of the Serbian dark comedy *Huddersfield* premiered as a TUTA production at Victory Gardens Theatre in Chicago this summer. Other recent premieres: *Iphigenia...a rave fable* at 7 Stages in Atlanta/GA, *Antigone Arkhe* at The Women's Project/NY (as part of *Antigone Project),* her translation of Garcia Lorca's *The House of Bernarda Alba* at the Pearl Theatre/NY, and her multimedia collaboration (with Todd Cerveris and Nick Philippou) *The Booth Variations* at 59 East 59th Street Theatre/NY and 2005 Edinburgh fringe festival/UK. Her dark comedy *Magnificent Waste* was selected by Tribeca Film Institute's All Access Open Stage program, and is also recipient of a National Latino Playwriting Award. Her version of Garcia Lorca's *Yerma* was recently developed as a music-theatre piece with composer Elizabeth Swados and director Kay Matschullat at NYU's HotInk Festival. She is listed in the *Oxford Encyclopedia of Latino History.*

Her translations of five plays and thirteen poems by Federico Garcia Lorca are published in *Impossible Theater* (Smith & Kraus). Play Publications: *Iphigenia...a rave fable* in *TheatreForum, Twelve Ophelias* (Kendall-Hunt Publishing and *CallReview), The Archaeology of Dreams* (Stage & Screen), *Gleaning/Rebusca* (Arte Publico Press), *Scar* (Third Woman Press), *Brazo Gitano* in *Ollantay Theater Journal. Fugitive Pieces (a play with songs), Luna Park and Any Place But Here* are published by Playscripts Inc. *Prodigal Kiss (a play with songs)* and *but there are fires* are published by Smith & Kraus.

Other credits: *Alchemy of Desire/Dead-Man's Blues* at the Cincinnati Playhouse in the Park (winner of the Rosenthal New Play Prize) under Lisa Peterson's direction, and *Any Place But Here* at Theater for the New City/NYC under Maria Irene Fornes' direction. *Fugitive Pieces* at Cleveland Public Theatre/OH, Kitchen Dog Theater in Dallas, Texas, and at Salvage Vanguard in Austin under Jason Neulander's direction, *The Archaeology of Dreams* at Portland Stage Company's Little Festival of the Unexpected, *Iphigenia...(a rave fable)* workshopped by Actors Touring Company/UK at the Euripides' Festival in Monodendri, Greece, and *Twelve Ophelias (a play with broken songs)* was presented at Baruch Performing Arts Center in New York.

She has held an NEA/TCG Residency at the Mark Taper Forum Theatre, and was resident playwright at INTAR Theatre in New York. She has been guest artist at the Traverse Theatre in Edinburgh, the Royal Court Theatre, and has taught playwriting at Yale School of Drama, Bennington College, Ohio State University, and the US-Cuba Writers' Conference in Havana. She is contributing editor of *TheatreForum*, is on the editorial board of *Contemporary Theatre Review* (Routledge/UK), and founder of NoPassport. She holds an MFA from UCSD, and is resident playwright of New Dramatists. Her website is www.caridadsvich.com